ELEGY FOR THE OTHER WOMAN

selected and new
terribly female poems

Elisavietta Ritchie

SIGNAL BOOKS
Chapel Hill, NC

Also by Elisavietta Ritchie:

WILD GARLIC: THE JOURNAL OF MARIA X. (novella in verse) 1995

A WOUND-UP CAT AND OTHER BEDTIME STORIES
(poetry) 1993

FLYING TIME: STORIES AND HALF-STORIES (fiction) 1992, 1996

THE PROBLEM WITH EDEN (poetry) 1985

RAKING THE SNOW (poetry) 1982

MOVING TO LARGER QUARTERS (poetry) 1977

A SHEATH OF DREAMS AND OTHER GAMES (poetry) 1976

TIGHTENING THE CIRCLE OVER EEL COUNTRY
(poetry) 1974

TIMBOT (novella in verse) 1971

Anthologies edited:

THE DOLPHIN'S ARC: POEMS ON ENDANGERED
CREATURES OF THE SEA   1989

FINDING THE NAME   1983

Translations:

THE TWELVE, by Aleksandr Blok 1968

"Glows with the right word in the absolutely right place, unerringly chosen to set the mood and tone. Hints of Dostoyevsky and the families of Tolstoy in the works of a woman of today! Provacative!"

Mary Sue Koeppel, *Kalliope: A Journal of Women's Art*

"I read *Flying Time* with enormous enjoyment. It reveals delicate witchery and a teeming imagination....I was crossing horizons of the spirit."

D.M. Thomas, author of *The White Hotel*

"Elisavietta Ritchie delivers: language that makes music in your head, haunting images that cut close to the bone, wonderfully authentic explorations of a wide range of human experiences. She weaves a magical world that will draw you back again and again."

Sandra Martz, Editor, Papier Mâché Press

"All good poets cannot write good prose, but Lisa Ritchie can. The sharply observed details, the detached but intimate voice, the subtle grasp of emotional configurations of these stories and memoirs glow like the blue and gold domes of Russian churches."

Lloyd Van Brunt, *Poems New and Selected 1962-1992*

On *Tightening The Circle Over Eel Country*, winner, Great Lakes Colleges Association's New Writer's Prize, Best First Book of Poetry 1975-76:

"Elisavietta Ritchie's poetry combines a byzantine elegance with straightforward plain style honesty. The extraordinary range of her interests—work, love, sensuality, and man's plight in a forlorn civilization -— is reinforced by her exquisite regard for language and a lively fascination with the possibilities of form."

William Packard, *New York Quarterly*

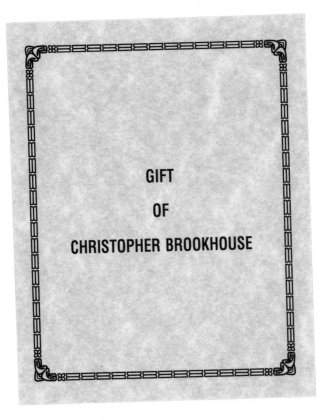

ELEGY FOR THE OTHER WOMAN

Illustrations by Jennifer Miller

Cover and book design by Michael Brown

Photograph by Clyde Henri Farnsworth

Printed in the USA

Library of Congress Cataloguing-in Publication Data

Ritchie, Elisavietta
ELEGY FOR THE OTHER WOMAN:
Selected and New Terribly Female Poems / Elisavietta Ritchie

ISBN 930095-20-0

1. Title

Signal Books
Suite 26
The Courtyard
431 W. Franklin St.
P.O. Box 1210
Chapel Hill, NC, 27514
Phone (919) 929-5985
1-800-266-5204
Fax: (919)-929-5986

Dedicated to The Other Woman,

with a peculiar gratitude

ACKNOWLEDGMENTS

The author is grateful to the following publications, wherein certain poems in this book first appeared, often in earlier or prose versions:

"Advice Column," published as "Old Flame, or Portrait of a Woman of Action," in *Pulpsmith; Lite Year '86*; and in its present version in *Singles Magazine; A Wound-Up Cat And Other Bedtime Stories,* Palmerston Press, © 1993 by the author; *Flying Time: Stories & Half-Stories,* Signal Books, © 1992 and 1996 by the author.

"Advice For A Daughter": *New York Quarterly,* 1995; *Hungry As We Are: Twentieth Anniversary Anthology,* ed. Ann Darr, Washington Writers Publishing House, 1995.

"After A Wedding": *The Problem With Eden,* Armstrong State College Press, © 1985 by the author.

"An Editor Asks Me To Consider Substituting 'Seed' for 'Sperm'": *Stone Country,* 1984.

"Bargains": *Passager,* 1994.

"Cautionary Tale For A Daughter": *Poet Lore,* 1993.

"Challenges": *Lite Year '86; The Problem With Eden.*

"Christine and Me": *A Sheath of Dreams And Other Games,* Proteus Press, © 1976 by the author.

"Clearing The Path": *When I Am An Old Woman I Shall Wear Purple,* ed. Sandra Martz; *Belles Lettres; The Problem With Eden; Flying Time: Stories & Half-Stories; Each In Her Own Way,* ed. Elizabeth Clamans, Queen of Swords Press, 1993; *The Arc of the Storm,* Signal Books, © 1996 by the author.

"Curse Poem For The Woman Who Shoved Her Shopping Cart Ahead Of Mine At The Check-Out": *The New York Times; A Wound-Up Cat And Other Bedtime Stories.*

"Economic Measures": *Raking The Snow,* The Washington Writers Publishing House, 1982; *Modernsense; Word-of-Mouth; Flying Time: Stories & Half-Stories.*

"Education": *Domestic Disobedience,* ed. Elizabeth Clamans; *A Wound-Up Cat And Other Bedtime Stories; Amelia* (won Galbraith award).

"Elegy For The Other Woman": *New York Quarterly; Woman As Is,* ed. William Packard, Dell Books, 1996; *The Unicorn and The Garden,* ed. Betty Parry; *What's A Nice Girl Like You Doing In A Relationship Like This,* ed. Kay Porterfield; *Uncle; Off My Face; Raking The Snow; Flying Time: Stories & Half-Stories; The Arc of the Storm; Lite Year '97.*

"Finale": *eleven.*

"For A Jealous Suitor, Getting On": *Amelia.*

"Free Falling": © *The Christian Science Monitor.*

"Holding For The Poles": as "Yo-Yo," in *Kalliope: a journal of women's art*, Vol. 15, No. 3, Fall 1993.

"Mail Call: After Long Absence": © 1993, *The New York Times*.

"The Mother of the Famous Man": *Women Celebrate Breaking Silence Into Joy,* ed. Elizabeth Welles, 1996.

"One Wedding Night": *Kalliope: a journal of women's art,* Fall 1994.

"The Poet as Playgirl: A Naked Dream Poem": *Georgetown Scholar*; *Tightening The Circle Over Eel Country*, Acropolis Books, © 1974 by the author.

"Recipe": *New York Quarterly*; *Light*; *Raking The Snow*.

"Report From The Stratosphere": *Kalliope: a journal of women's art,* Vol. 15, No. 3, Fall 1993.

"Savings & Thrift": © 1986 *The New York Times*; *eleven*; *Excaliber*; *MPS Bulletin*; *Stone Soup Gazette*; *A Wound-Up Cat and Other Bedtime Stories*.

"A Secret Admirer Sends Me An Antique Venetian Greeting Card": *Amelia* (won Starbuck award); reprinted in a review.

"Strawberries": *Flying Time: Stories & Half-Stories*.

"Taking Stock on New Year's Night": *Home Planet News*; *Flying Time: Stories &Half-Stories*; *Each In Her Own Way*;

"Urban Services": *Footwork,* 1984; *Flying Time: Stories & Half-Stories*.

"Wedding Ring Waltz": *New York Quarterly* 1992.

"You Ask If I've Met The Famous Writer": *Second Glance,* 1994.

The author expresses her gratitude for encouragement and help from:
The PEN Syndicated Fiction Project for four awards;
The DC Commission for the Arts and Humanities for four Individual Artist Grants;
The Virginia Center for the Creative Arts for several fellowships;
Colleen Perrin of The Palmerston Press, Toronto;
The Washington Writers Publishing House.
And for their editorial and proofreading assistance:
Clyde Henri Farnsworth, Suzanne Collins, Maxine Combs, Mary Edsall, Elizabeth Follin-Jones, Ann Knox, Jim Nason, Roxanne Henderson, and especially Dougald McMillan of Signal Books.

CONTENTS

I. CLEARING THE PATH

II. ADVICE FOR A DAUGHTER

III. SAVINGS & THRIFT

I

CLEARING THE PATH

ELEGY FOR THE OTHER WOMAN

May her plane explode
with just one fatality.
But, should it not,
may the other woman spew
persistent dysentery
from your first night ever after.
May the other woman vomit
African bees and Argentine wasps.
May cobras uncoil from her loins.
May she be eaten not
by something dramatic like lions,
merely by a homely warthog.
I do not want her to fall down a well
for fear of spoiling the water
nor die on the highway because
she might obstruct traffic.
Rather, something easy, and cheap:
clap contracted en route from some other bloke.
And should she nonetheless survive
all these critical possibilities
may she quietly die of boredom with you.

ADVICE COLUMN

When your lover invites you to join him
at dinner with his old flame
who just blew into town,

Wear your barest black dress,
unwrap black lace stockings,
slip on sandals with gold spike heels.

Choose the jewelry which
is unmistakably real,
preferably his most recent gift.

Curl your hair, kohl your eyes,
knowing you're not as young as you used to be.
You hope she is even older.

Stock your purse
with expensive perfume,
an avant-garde shade of lipstick,

and mad money enough
to send you all home
in separate cabs.

You wonder if you should be
the first to arrive
at the medium-priced cafe,

or give them a chance
to talk. You decide
this once you will not be late.

You forget you are nursing
a fever. Perhaps
she will catch it too.

You file your nails to a point,
button your long black gloves
and sally into the dark.

CLEARING THE PATH

My husband gave up shovelling snow
at forty-five because, he claimed,
that's when heart attacks begin.

Since it snowed regardless I,
mere forty, took the shovel, dug.
Now fifty, still it falls on me

to clean the walk. He's gone on
to warmer climes and younger loves
who will, I guess, keep shovelling for him.

In other seasons here, I sweep
plum petals or magnolia cones
to clear the way for heartier loves.

URBAN SERVICES

1 a.m. I almost crash against
the possum carcass in the street
before the old house of my old
husband's new wife. I'm terribly
sad about the possum all smashed up.
Needle teeth and nose have lost
their point, greywhite fur is torn
and wet, blood across the asphalt.
I don't like being on the street
at 1 a.m., but the Police have no
desire to cart off carcasses at 1 a.m.
despite the risk of causing wrecks,
Just phone Sanitation at 8 a.m., Lady.
So here I am at 1 a.m., dead possums,
lively muggers and no police protection
nor rubber gloves. But I pick up
the coil of rubber tail, guide nose end
inside a plastic bag and tie a knot.
The nearest supercan happens to stand
in front of his old mistress' old house
already full of trash so it sticks out
beneath the lid. May be a week before
the Trash Department rumbles past,
so what if it turns a bit inside
its grave, I am dancing on mine.

CURSE POEM FOR THE WOMAN WHO SHOVED HER SHOPPING CART AHEAD OF MINE AT THE CHECKOUT

May your ice cream curdle,
your eggs explode,
molasses leak,
yogurt spot.

May your fancy salmon
have a toad in its throat,
your caviar turn
into buckshot.

May the wheels of your cart
catch on the curb,
cherries roll all over
the parking lot.

May your bags hatch weevils,
your cartons—moths.
May beetles rumble,
roaches trot

from the store
to your house
to your room,
and everything rot.

And may your check bounce.

TAKING STOCK ON NEW YEAR'S NIGHT

Tonight my failing father asks
is it true I am pregnant
I shake my head but he can't see

One blue-flowered gingham dove
dropped from the Christmas tree
reminds me I'm no longer a stuffed duck

Rather a sailor granted liberty in Rio
the only admonition being
remember galoshes

No clocks or calendars or globes
warn me where I am
or ought to be

Gold-rimmed and chipped
dishes sit in the fetid sink
with garlic peels and feta crumbs

The swelling black-and-white cat
licks my wrist as if I shared
in her complicity

HEATING PROBLEMS

Last night, pipes burst.
Freeze, thaw, freeze.
In the broken farmhouse
rugs drip over frames of chairs
soaked to the bone.

I bail gallons before
the plumber arrives,
stubbled from answering
the whole county's
emergency calls.

He cases the house,
crawls under the cellar,
even onto the roof:
Everywhere leaks.
Puddles freeze, and my pails.

Two hours later he leaves
with my check for $150,
our prayers it won't bounce,
and since this is New Year's Eve
my only bottle of Mumm's.

Tonight, in a building
I suppose we own (in dreams
one assumes so much),
he returns, shaven clean,
pulls me across his lap,

rubs my back, and much more
lies ahead but I roll away
as pipes burst all over the house
and only I seem to know
where to turn off the valves.

CHALLENGES

My boarder's new girl, a zippy brunette,
looks me over as I emerge
from the cellar.

I have lived here 23 years
and carried 23 x 365 loads
of laundry up these dim steps,

but tonight my arms only hold
a bottle of elderly wine
and two silver goblets.

My boarder is younger than
my own son, yet I sense
his girlfriend senses a rival.

My hair and my teeth
are my own and my stockings
are black, and lace.

"And who are you?" she demands.
"What's your function here
in this crazy place?"

I ponder her question, then
look her square: "I run
this establishment."

ECONOMIC MEASURES

1.
You'd be proud how I'm thrifty with liquor now:
only one drop stains the brandy glass.

When guests look surprised, I explain: I killed
the bishop. Or at least, after I poured his snifter

brimful with your best Armagnac, Drambuie,
whatever flask studded with stars,

my instincts generous, innocent, but
you were aghast at the waste,

the next year the bishop died. Already alcoholic,
far off, yet you blamed me for the crime.

2.
Later the antique lute, your final anniversary gift—
was it meant to play out the forthcoming dance of divorce?—

fell and broke, I was also at fault although
when it crashed I was three towns away to the north.

That same day you discovered
my tiny black kitten squashed in the ruts of a car.

You accused me of that murder too even when
our neighbor in tears proved it was her Peugeot.

3.
Now you've left. I ration each drop of my life,
barely sprinkle kirsch over the fruit.

I keep kittens in, neighbors out,
lutes wired to the wall.

All is sober, stingy and silent now.
I avoid any risks

except those of love. Here
I am profligate, and it floods.

II

ADVICE FOR A DAUGHTER

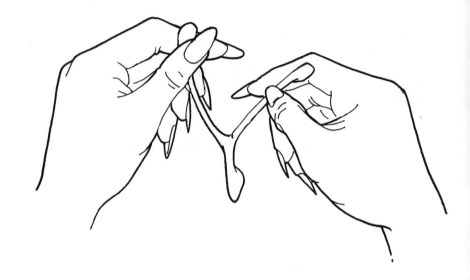

ADVICE FOR A DAUGHTER

Do not gnaw chicken bones before
a lover, I tell her, as we crunch
the cartilege of a hapless hen.

Could put him off, give rise
to thoughts you might have
taste for more than skin.

My lover is so meticulous
he uses knife and fork,
misses deep pleasures.

I have to sneak to the kitchen,
chew both our drumsticks clean
before I scrape the plates.

The best is what some call
the parson's nose, others term
the pope's, the rabbi's.

My mother said: What scuttles
through the fence the last
is surely the most succulent.

So while our chicken stews apart
you and I retrieve the bubbling bones,
gnaw, juices trickling down our chins,

and weigh the risks of loss:
either a fastidious lover
or the choice parts of a bird.

CAUTIONARY TALE FOR A DAUGHTER

As for passions: yes, I know
all the grand insanities
first-hand....Dear girl, don't
despair. There is always

a dashing Gypsy outside the gate
with a knife-grinding wheel.
His molten tin waits to repair
every hole in your home.

You hear his bell down the road,
his fiddle which makes you dance.
Guess how he'll look
twenty years hence.

And the Transylvanian prince
flashing his gems and his eyes
who turns out to be the head
waiter au Bistro d'Auverne.

The Delta squire
whose mansion sank
in the swamp: nowadays
hens are his thoroughbreds.

The artist with sable lashes,
eyes pools of aquarelles caked
on a palette; he could use a new
model, has used up a score.

The man once tall and thin
as a loblolly pine,
whose mind ran even faster
than yours and who,

after thirteen years a gnarled oak,
remains avid for you, skilled
from practice with all your friends,
and now weighs two-hundred-fifty.

Lined up behind the spiraea, they
break branches of deathwhite blooms
to weave no bridal bouquets,
only wreaths....Whom will you choose?

SARTORIAL CONSIDERATIONS

I'd never run off to Manhattan with a man
who wears green double-knit polyester suits
and yellowish ties, and while the one

who invited me—he'd choose a hotel
with a pool—leads an exciting life as a spy
nabbing dictators, terrorists and Red Guards,

might be my choice on safari
or sharing an iceberg with polar bears,
and his IQ could get him in MENSA,

he wasn't quite smart enough to suspect
that a woman like me prefers lovers
in herringbone tweeds, paisley foulards,

best of all, black sweater and corduroys,
an old scarf wound thrice round the throat,
ends waving, waving. At least in Manhattan.

THE SAFEST LOVE AFFAIR

She sleeps with windows wide.
Not that she loves the Arctic air.
Even on a moonless night she won't
shut away the stars, rain, hail

or lightning flash that bounces off
the growling clouds. A modest moth,
emboldened gnat, can always find
the split inch of her window screen.

He locks his windows, lines his drapes,
draws them tight. No headlights pierce
venetian blinds, cast dangerous calligraphs.
Air conditioners roar lullabies of steel.

How they'll resolve this if not clear:
The story ought to run its course
from paragraph to paragraph,
from yellow rose to final kiss.

The safest love affairs are those
which don't proceed beyond
the proclamation of the eyes,
the message of the fingertips.

Could it be best he stays inside
his shuttered house, while she awaits
cecropia moths and splendid nights
of hurricanes and flooding moons.

A SECRET ADMIRER SENDS ME
AN ANTIQUE VENETIAN GREETING CARD

He pictures me in a gondola
in billowy skirts of green,
white bodice made for unlacing,
wings in my curls,
lashes downcast,
inviting as sherbet in June.

Our two discreet gondoliers
in red knickers, duncecaps and vests,
candy-striped sleeves
afloat in the breeze,
pole over waves of watered desire.

Perhaps they will steer us out
into the Adriatic.
Perhaps they will rob and dump us
in a canal at dusk.

Whatever our fate, this autumn day
mischievous, warm as a gypsy's hand,
the gondoliers bellow their arias,
he hums *obbligati* into my ears,
and our curved barque
is drifting seaward too fast.

But his velvet jacket
more blue than the dubious waves
and stiff white ruff
prickle my skin,

and I've never before kissed a man
who kept his hat on,
even a cap of cerulean satin.

TRANSMOGRIFICATIONS

I rush for the plane—
always I'm late—holes
in my sneakers and jeans,

backpack—my daughter's—slung
on my shoulder, scuffed duffle
spilling racquets and boom-box.

At her age I travelled in sensible
navyblue dress, hat and heels,
white gloves. My luggage matched.

In childhood didn't I
secretly fear growing up
and becoming my mother?

Do I instead grow
more with each year
like my daughter?

In the duty-free shop
I buy Bailey's Irish Cream,
a concoction I loved, adolescent.

Among perfume testers
I spot one pale flask.
Shalimar! My mother's favorite.

"Could I try a splash?"
The duty-free lady entrusts me
with the whole tester.

I test until the shop lures
throngs of bees, and men
buying four-star cognacs

sniff me with hope
or at least admiration.
Yet Shalimar, while genteel,

is pallid. So are Blue Grass,
Muguets and Chanel.
Then like my daughter I pick

amber flagons, dangerous names:
Opium, Poison, the hard-core stuff.
Airborne, I'll find a new lover.

BARGAINS ON SHUTTLE FLIGHTS

He smiles at me across the aisle
like a rug merchant
with 1001 other lines

seldom far from his mind
though he cannot expect success
with every potential client,

the intent is perennial
as the signs plastered over his store:
LOST LEASE! FIRE SALE! EVERYTHING OFF!

I smile back though not in the market
for a marked-down rug or merchant
or rolling around on piled carpets—

Kermanshah, Bokhara, Sarouk, Tabriz—
fragrant with frankincense, myrrh
and moth-proofing. Still, despite frayed

fringes, worn warps and woofs,
and a slight creakiness of the loom,
neither of us is yet a valued antique.

But the FASTEN SEAT BELTS sign is on
and I get giddy on flying carpets,
am allergic to wool.

III

SAVINGS & THRIFT

MAIL CALL : AFTER LONG ABSENCE

Each envelope brings threats:

one will cut the water off by noon,
a second, douse the lights, stop time,
another, disconnect the sewer pipe.

No more utility in my utilities:
every card in this Monopoly
leads straight to jail.

The only heat left is on me.
The bank warns of foreclosure,
dispossession of my car.

American Express and Mastercard
shine plastic countenances
full of usury and menace.

No more safety in numbers
nor bulls in the marketplace.
And all my memberships have lapsed.

PAINTING LENA'S PLACE

Must quit today at three,
sighs my curly auburn-haired painter
with the winning grin
and Scottish lilt to his tales,

a fortnight behind as he tries
to mask the cracked apricot
walls of previous tenants
with absolute white for me

while I try to survive amid cartons,
a disaster of furniture heaped,
endless cans of plaster and paint,
no room to move, though I've moved in.

True, he's patched and sanded and painted
twelve-hour days, deserves one evening off
to launder his shorts, watch TV. I
have no time for that, can't even unpack.

I add an extra inch of milk to his tea,
warm him a muffin, real butter, while
we exchange more dabs of our lives.
Yes, tonight he must help his friend Lena,

she's the girl lived here before, she liked
these apricot walls, did him favors, now
he's promised to paint her new flat,
it'll just take a couple of nights.

He leers past his brush. "But— but— "
I stutter, "But what about my—"
I stare at his wild oily curls laced
with grey hairs, splattered with paint.

As for Lena, I picture her a peach
from the supermarket: rock-hard all week,
then overnight sponge-soft, rotten spots,
still hard round the pit, tasting of turpentine.

EDUCATION

"Boys or girls?" asks the evangelist
as he counts out my bloodworms,
a full baker's dozen, squirming.
His plump elbow jabs mine.

I reel my mind back
to Miss Campbell's Biology class.
In 12th Grade she unveiled
fetal pigs in formaldehyde,

and one girl whispered
they're babies, aborted.
"But worms," I recall,
"are hermaphrodites—"

The preacher leans against dusty packets
of sinkers and hooks on the shelf
with Beechnut chewing tobacco, pints
of Four Roses, week-old Wonder bread.

"I've asked that many a time.
You're the first with the right answer."
He looks me over, is he weighing my soul?
Then: "Do attend my revival meeting tonight...."

I wonder: is he anxious to save my soul
or continue my sex education?
I thank him, pay for my bloodworms,
go off to the dock after perch.

AN EDITOR ASKS ME TO CONSIDER
SUBSTITUTING "SEED" FOR "SPERM"

I've no problem being
euphemistic. Just *being...*
Or would have had
had there not been

one elusive and errant
wiggly smart-alec
well-programmed tad-
pole homing in.

Animal, not
vegetal. Not
agrarian. Marine.
Unless you imagine

a maple seed
with wings
fluttering down
to a puddle

and, after a pleasant sail,
floating beneath the waves
like a tired flying fish
or a dead squid.

If it indeed
had been a seed,
I might now be an oak.
Or more likely, fig.

I seem to remain
perpetually wet
like my daddy-half
swimming upstream

or unwittingly paddling
my leaky kayak
against a tide
of censorship.

THE POET AS PLAYGIRL:
A NAKED DREAM POEM

Last night I dreamed
I posed for *Playboy*, not
in my Maidenform bra.

I lolled upon a white fur rug
like my angora cat in her white heat
meowling for the bored photographers.

Enough of scoured psyches,
murky symbols couched
in rhyme obliquely.

Just a touch
of deft chiaroscuro
to prove I'm art.

Good for once to *be*
instead of merely *meaning*.
Now I was sprung, and not my rhyme.

Still living, young, I've won
my immortality,
all three dimensions fixed in two,

ignoring elements of time—
which does show minor ravages,
too many midnight rapings by the muse.

For the duration of my dream
I undulated, froze
in metaphysic poses,

each blue-white flash illuminating
lines, myself a pulsing image now,
a living metaphor.

YOU ASK IF I'VE MET THE FAMOUS WRITER

I've yet to meet him in the flesh
but yes, I intend to read him.

Should we meet corporeally I will
caress the lobes of his famous ears.

In the photograph on his dust jacket—
in my house, an apt adjective—

his Adonic profile shows only one ear:
was the other lost in a literary scuffle?

I'll trace my fingers over his lips
parted in half-smile, ironic, dyspeptic,

graze his skin, wrinkles of wisdom around
those insightful eyes, surely sapphire,

then stroke that broad brow, hope
to stoke his furnace of inspiration.

When at last we meet in the flesh
we will fit together like a Chinese

three-dimensional puzzle, all parts
interlocked, surface continuous, smooth.

But I was always impatient with puzzles,
though elderly aunts, to improve my mind,

brought them whenever I had a cold.
I donated them all to the school bazaar.

So I fear in our passion we might insert
the wrong pieces in the wrong niches, concave

into convex, end up not a sphere but a multi-armed
bodhisattva, or a Northwest Indian totem pole.

And what lurks below his dubious neck
may be lean and hard as a wooden puzzle,

as intricate and frustrating....Yet since
that book is old, six chins might reside

beneath his heroic jaw, reservoirs of jowls
in chiaroscuro or five-o'clock shadow,

and, both flabby, we'd lump together
like bean bags or sacks of flour.

Or, like porcupines careless in love, we might
stick quills in each other's soft sectors.

What a gamut of juxtapositions
could flesh out our historic encounter!

Meanwhile, I promise to praise his books,
look out for him in the flesh.

THE FRENCH NOVELIST

She reads her story
describing the lover
meeting her in the cafe,

how he kissed his way down
the slide of her spine
in black split-back dress,

how in the park in the night
in the rain in the passion
her hands slithered into his jeans

and how at last oh at last
he stuck his shaft in her
through next she calls it a scythe—

Although she depicts all this
with magnificent eloquence,
I keep expecting a surprise

punch line, revelation the lover
was a woman, a horse or a bear,
something kinky, a jolt, or joke.

But she slides into the afterwards'
Great Satisfaction in the park
in the night in the rain.

That's the whole story, purple prose
in a plain envelope, she is please
to relate on stage with such daring.

But I think: *God, lady, if it were
really so great, you could not,
you could not, describe it.*

SAVINGS & THRIFT

I buy clothes second-hand,
haunt Goodwill for plates,
yard sales for chairs,
rent ramshackle houses,
invest in used cars.
My lovers also
have seen better days.
But what bargains I find...

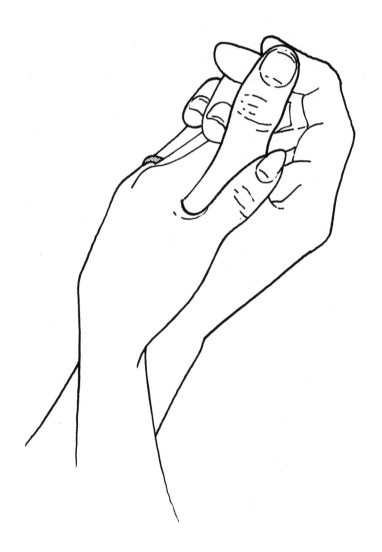

IV

WEDDING RING WALTZ

AFTER A WEDDING

Last week I caught
my first bridal bouquet.
Like a cold, unintended.

Twelve white carnations
wired stiff into lace
around one striped lily

aggressively red,
a starfish embracing
oysters. The whole bunch

flipped over the heads
of six bridesmaids
and other nubiles,

into my face.
My hands
had to catch it.

My neighbor Amanda,
like me after years
suddenly single, is bitter.

She'd have liked
a crack at it. But she
was off eating the cake.

I clipped one sprig
which she pinned
in her hair like a girl.

She seemed pacified.
"Furthermore," I offered,
"when I marry whomever,

I'll let you borrow him
some Thursday nights."
I am still waiting.

But so is Amanda.

BARGAINS

Did parsimony begin when my mother
insisted redheads should not wear red,
so she bought me dresses in avocado,
ochre and brown, too well-sewn to wear out.

She fitted me into glistening oxfords
when scuffed saddle shoes or loafers
with pennies were in. At the prom,
ridiculous ruffles covered my throat.

Always I've bought the Edsel,
off-brand computers that won't compat,
thrift shop clothes with the ghosts
of their owners still playing tricks.

I've rented old houses that slip apart
beam by beam, bought third-hand boats
and fibreglassed porous hulls
while mice spun the sails into lace.

For my second wedding I've bought
second-hand silver spike heels
and a décolleté pink faille dress.
My hair is a staunch apricot.

I've landed this curious bridegroom,
a hand-me-down too, but game
to travel cut-rate with me.
Still, I worry a bit.

WEDDING RING WALTZ

The ring barely slips over
my swollen third-finger joint (broke
on a long-ago boat), slides round
the thin inside inch of my finger.

Mum's wedding ring. I wear hers
because my bridegroom does not
believe in symbols, or he lacked
time to shop, or the cash.

Yet aren't we regardless
always more tied to our mothers
than to whatever spouses.... This could
spring into a psychological novel,

dangerous, concentric, drag on
for tomes. Therefore best I wind up
the topic in sixteen lines, go
soap my hands, wrest off the ring.

ONE WEDDING NIGHT

He blinks to note the old
woman parked in his bed

all wrinkles and bellies, breasts
not as full as they seemed.

Which psychological drive, she
wonders, pushed her to sleep

with this grandfather figure,
and what if, in the midst

of things, his heart fails?
What would the rescue squad—

those husky bucks—speculate?
Not the usual bimbo here

who makes an old man's pump
seize up when he tries—

He turns down, she turns
off, the unkind light.

In silence they strive
to ignore imperfections,

remember the rules,
at least work around them,

holding each other
lightly as luna moths.

RECIPE: ONE ARTICHOKE

Hold me
tightly or
I'll roll free.

Slice through my spines.
Though I cry, show no mercy:
remember sea urchins.

Heat me up an hour
among lemons, bay leaves,
peppercorns, salt.

Pry with care.
When at last
I spread a bit

peel me leaf by leaf,
bathe me
in hot butter,

scrape my softness off
with greedy teeth.
Discard thistles.

Beneath your knife
my heart waits. But
eat me slowly.

DINNERTIME

Two filets of salmon
side by side marinate
in briny seas and sauce

until our last
resistant bones
dissolve

poach over low flames
or fiercely broil
ruddy pink

serve
with a wedge
of lime

V

FREE-FALLING

HOLDING FOR THE POLES

And the end of all our exploring
Will be to arrive where we started
　　　　　T.S. Eliot, *Four Quartets*

Despite intentions
I always flash
back to myself

Even when I set out
to explore afar
something's askew

I turn up in the Amazon
wearing my Arctic parka
boots like elephant legs

Or head for the Poles
in spiked sandals, sarong
faded from too many

moons which seem new
one moment an orange
the next an egg

but it's the same
half-scraped potato
dependant on how

you slice it
No matter how
I stretch toward the sky

wherever I go
dirt lurks
beneath my nails

AGAINST GIVING ME A LIGHTER

Don't want to give fire to a poet.
Here's my compass instead.
                    Alexander Ritchie

But mine is not
a life for those
who navigate.

I cannot plot
a watered course
toward either pole
nor read the stars.

Here on earth
I zigzag up
and down
a twisting path.

Still, at the top
I'll have my fire.

FREE–FALLING

"Oh, are you the sky diver
we're expecting today?
The captain from the parachute corps?"

The head of the Speakers Committee
beams as I lug my bag
of poems to the podium.

Parachutist? Perhaps...
Though only a fool would jump
unless his plane were on fire,

I leap from altitudes
I'd not thought to reach
into terrain

unmapped, unknown.
So far my chute
has blossomed in time.

THE MOTHER OF THE FAMOUS MAN

after seeing *A River Runs Through It,*
then *Long Day's Journey Into Night*

In his autobiography, also the notes
others kept, the profiles they wrote,
and especially the version on film,
she never does much but cook, bring meals
to table—soup, roast, pie gashed like a wound—
and ask why someone picks at his food.
She smiles for the camera, waves as the horse
disappears down the road, weeps over loss.

In short: self-effacing, applesweet, brave.
Or—in some other son's script—bitter, betrayed.
Medusa, dragon, a silent or wild alcoholic,
frantically knitting, tacitly menopausal.
Fat as a bun or gaunt as a rusted pipe,
how nicely we fit in our stereotypes.

Watch out, when they get to the book and film on *my*
sons, for a Kali: eight arms, great breasts,
                              a perpetual smile.

CHRISTINE AND ME

Already men meld in my mind.
I grow old and forget
a shocking tally of loves.

Yet think of Christine Keeler,
shunted to Old Bailey for Profumo's trial,
then from courthouse back to limousine,

face lovely, pancake-masked behind
the window glass, daily flashbulbed,
flashbulbed, terrified.

Biddies in an avid ring
cling to fenders, handles, hood,
like wasp eggs laid

beneath the skin of caterpillars
undulant and succulent
to hatch and feed upon.

And they whisper to one another,
"At least she's lived, dearie."
"She's lived life to the full, the bitch."

FOR A JEALOUS SUITOR, GETTING ON:
a ragged sonnet

The verb to love has no past tense.
Konstantin Simonov

I mention old lovers. You envision
wheelchairs, walkers and canes, a battalion
who bob, hawk, and hobble up my worn stairs,
saliva ignored on their birdnest beards.

A properly comic scene. Not yet true
but I trust my seasoned loves will endure
as they do now, across oceans and years
at least in *my* mind. Don't let them haunt yours:

The best of the lot are already dead.
"The body's tyranny," one artist said.
Not sure then which part he meant, now I find
the body's treachery outstrips the mind's.

So I'm relieved your eyesight's feebler than
your memory. And glad you're still on hand.

REPORT FROM THE STRATOSPHERE

Travel ahead, reads my horoscope.
A frequent flyer with no boarding pass,
airsick on rougher flights,
I finger the warty globe, hesitate.

Travel ahead. Verb or noun? Safer than
backward travel, paddling into the past
in my leaky canoe, or tacking my iceboat
against the wind over a crumpled pond.

Travel ahead, always ahead, instructions
cackle from the socked-in control tower.
Ignoring iced wings, weather reports, war zones,
at last I taxi into the blizzard

punching buttons, spinning knobs,
clutching the stick, clutching the clutch,
clutching whatever might weigh me down—
Scattering maps, I soar beyond orbit.

VI

STRAWBERRIES

STRAWBERRIES

Who comforts the undiscovered
lover who mourns in secret
beyond familial circles of grief.

I was discreet.
Your widow never knew.

Or did that bone sense
those of us who are wives
seem to acquire with the ring,

premonition we'll lose our man
an occasional night, at least one
unguarded afternoon before
Death turns his trick,
did it warn her of a parallel force?

Men cherish first loves, they say,
but especially their last.
You came midway through
my spectrum, but I
fell at your rainbow's end.

Your pot of gold
to barter with Death
was fast running out.

That May, too late in your life
whose limits were set (mine
promised to stretch forever),
over strawberries, first of the year,
we discovered we'd rather
feast on each other.

Then we found we share
the same birthday,
promised our next one together:
a strawberry picnic by tropical seas.

You gave me sketches,
sparked my new poems.
How many more
might we have inspired?

No time, with late love,
to go stale. By now
one is too wise to get caught.

The Peruvian nurse
who oversaw your last days
along with your wife,
attentive as I could not be,

brought me your black briefcase,
sketchbook and old red chair
when your wife directed them out
to the curb with the trash.

Granted the case would not lock,
the leather was scuffed,
your drawings were rough,
the chair needed recovery.

Had you told the nurse about me?

Long nights while family slept
she doled out your pills
and the overripe strawberries

left on your doorstep—
who could pinpoint
which neighbor stopped by,
no guests allowed anymore—

in your delirium did you tattle,
betray? Or simply whisper,
Deliver these, por favor.

Did she just understand?
She knew about partings.
Did *she* close your eyes?
Or did sleep duplicate itself in the dark?

Each birthday since, I celebrate.
Unwitting friends fill in.
I toast you in silence,
strawberries in my champagne.

A decade gone, the red chair
still holds your shape.
Your sketches hold mine
in this briefcase covered
with moth wings and dust.
Summers, heat glues our pages.
Winters, mice nibble edges.

This early May, buzzards fly over
rows of strawberries ready to pick
when our birthday falls.

Why did you die just before?

Will I too, here in your chair,
while sketches and poems
burst from a briefcase
I cannot close?

FINALE

No farewells.
A slippery gypsy,
I'm off through the fog
trailing a tangle of rags
and a tarnished chain.

DATE DUE

GAYLORD   PRINTED IN U.S.A.

Elisavietta Ritchie's fiction, poetry, creative non-fiction, and translations from Russian and French have appeared in *Poetry, American Scholar, New York Times, Christian Science Monitor, Washington Post, Kalliope, Confrontation, New Letters, Nimrod, Calyx, Iris, Canadian Women's Studies, Epoch, Press, When I'm An Old Woman I Shall Wear Purple, If I Had My Life To Live Over, Grow Old Along With Me/The Best Is Yet To Be, The Tie That Binds, Gifts Of The Fathers, Diamonds Are A Girl's Best Friend, Two Worlds Walking,* and numerous other publications.